The "Poor Me" Manual

The "Poor Me" Manual

Perfecting Self-Pity—My Own Story

Hunter Lewis

Axios Press
PO Box 457
Edinburg, VA 22824
888.542.9467   info@axiosinstitute.org

Library of Congress Cataloging-in-Publication Data

Lewis, Hunter.
      The poor me manual : perfecting self-pity, my own story / by
Hunter Lewis.
      pages cm
      ISBN 978-1-60419-074-8 (hardcover)
      1. Emotions. 2. Happiness. 3. Success. 4. Conduct of life.
I. Title.

BF531.L46 2013
158.1--dc23

2013020142

Contents

Dedicated to my children.

Author's Note

One crisp sunny morning I was surprised to find a package left at my front door containing this book in manuscript form. Its author included a note saying that his last name was Lewis, that he had seen a book of mine, and that he had decided to adopt my name as his own. In addition, he expected me to publish his (our) book and that the cover should be "nice." I have tried to do as requested.

Introduction

PERFECTING SELF-PITY IS an unusual goal. But then I am an unusual person. Very occasionally unusual people attract followers. They change the way the world sees things, the way the world works. I am under no illusions that this book will find readers, or that if it does, anyone will want to follow my example. Perhaps at least some people will enjoy reading my story, regardless of whether it persuades them of anything.

As any reader will shortly learn, I have not always been of the same mind about almost anything. When young, I planned to be a stupendous, world-historical success. When all my hopes came crashing down in ruin, I explored other pathways.

My life has been rich in incident. When the French philosopher Montaigne heard a man say that he was a pathetic failure, he responded: "Have you not lived? Is that not the purpose of life?" This is not an exact quote, but Montaigne and I agree. I have lived. Indeed I may say that I have had an extraordinary life of exploration and discovery. If it was not successful by the world's standards, did it not give me this opportunity to nourish and perfect self-pity, and to share my accumulated insights with others?

Some will doubtless object that self-pity is too private a pleasure, or too selfish, or not robust enough. I may even be reviled like that poor fellow Machiavelli, whose only fault was describing people as they are, not as they pretend to be. The world rewarded him by making his first name, Nick, synonymous with the devil, and his last name with untrustworthy behavior. If I am not misunderstood or reviled, my position will strike most people as odd. Well, even I did not appreciate the dignity and truthfulness of self-pity until I was well into middle age.

Before proceeding with my life, which speaks for itself, let me note that if some readers see their way to sponsor pity parties, in order to promote this book, I would consider it a very thoughtful gesture.

Herewith my life in four acts, so to speak, with a concluding postlude.

The Green Years

I was young. I was ambitious. It wasn't just that I wanted to succeed. I had to succeed. It was a "must" situation. I couldn't be happy for a moment otherwise. Of course, one isn't supposed to admit this kind of thing. But why not? That's how I felt. Why pretend otherwise now?

1. My "Gamesman" Phase

I knew from observation that life is a game. There was no mystery about it. The object of the game is to outsmart and out-maneuver other people in order to win. Winning will get you whatever it is you want. What you should want is money, power, sex, fame, looking good, staying healthy. But above all, the real key is that you need to impress people.

As important as people are, you need to avoid being friends with them. Make them think they're your friend, sure. Get them to help you. But don't worry about loyalty and especially don't worry about keeping your promises.

You have to sound sincere; that's basic. But so long as you sound sincere when you make commitments, that's enough. Time will pass and you can always deny whatever it is you said. Get whatever you can out of other people and move on.

Alas, this approach did not work out as well as I expected. Through a real stroke of luck, my first college roommate was some kind of computer genius. He liked me and asked me to become his partner in selling the software he was developing. Then an unexpected systems server bill popped up. I would have had to help pay it from my allowance, and I promptly denied that we had ever agreed to be partners. My roommate moved out and on, became a multimillionaire in a few years, and all I had were the "might-have-beens" along with a lesson in the limitations of "gaming" my way through life.

2. My "Prince" Phase

I decided to take a different tack. Had I been born royalty, people would rush to do my bidding. Why not act as if I were royalty and make it clear that I expected to be waited upon, that whatever I wanted, I got?

I wouldn't be blatant about it. I would try my best to appear innocent, even charming. I was especially inspired by reading an essay describing Antoine de Saint-Exupéry, author of a famous illustrated little book named—what else?—*The Little Prince*. Here's an excerpt:

> [Exupéry was] a starry-eyed inno-
> cent [who] worked from midnight
> to seven in the morning and thought
> nothing of summoning his guests at
> any time to show off a drawing of
> which he was particularly proud....
> [Nor did he] hesitate to awaken his
> wife and the whole household, at
> two in the morning, to say that he
> was hungry, in dire need of a plate
> of scrambled eggs. In another two
> hours [he might call up the stairs]
> demand[ing] that his wife come
> down [to play] chess.*

I wasn't married yet, but tried the same tech-
nique on my girlfriend. It did not go smoothly.
That put me in a very bad mood. The next day
a friend refused to lend me money. Then, later
that same day, I was bumped from an over-
full airplane flight, despite having bought a

---

* Stacey Schiff, "A Grounded Soul: Saint-Exupéry in New York,"
New York Times Book Review, (May 30, 1993): 15.

ticket and traveled all the way to the airport. I demanded to be put on the plane, but the attendant wasn't buying it. I had to admit: Saint-Exupéry I wasn't.

3. My "High Flyer" Phase

Time was passing. I wasn't making my mark. I decided that I had to redouble my efforts, turn up the energy, do some high flying. Then I got another stroke of luck. I was hired as the personal assistant of the head of a brokerage firm. I wasn't the boss myself—not yet. But it was the next best thing—I spoke for the boss.

I was excited. I had a mission. I had prestige. I was determined to overcome obstacles and make things happen. I flew from project to project, department to department. I told them what the boss wanted done. I was amazing.

But then something remarkable happened. The department heads began to complain to the boss—about me! They, who didn't work half as hard, who had none of my enthusiasm, none of my buzz, none of my push, none of my creativity, dared to find fault with me. It couldn't be clearer that they were jealous.

The boss still liked me. He counseled me to slow down, be a little less impatient, suffer fools better, maybe concentrate on one thing. He reassigned me to head a new department selling real estate investments, which would keep me away from the other departments. I went at it broadside, worked sixteen hours a day, six or seven days a week.

I didn't make a sale during the first six months, but I knew sales were just around the corner, and I went into overdrive to get them. Nothing was going to stop me. I was so close to success that I could smell and taste it. Then the completely unexpected happened. Being overtired, I screamed at the head of computer operations in the hall one day, and the next day the boss fired me. I couldn't believe it. I stared at him speechless. I was on the verge of making it. I was the only one in the place with what it takes. I was going to have his job before long.

Maybe that was it. He probably felt threatened by me. He preferred to surround himself with mediocrities so that his own position would be safe.

Well, to heck with business, I thought. I decided to devote myself to doing good. Why not take on the hard one, I thought, so I decided to start a home for delinquent boys. I found a nice woman to put up some money and was off and running.

Or so I thought. Having bought a property, I needed to get the zoning board to approve its new use. I worked feverishly to put together a great presentation to the board, but then all the neighbors trooped in and started complaining. This old lady from across the street said she wouldn't feel safe and the comments were all downhill from there.

I couldn't believe my ears. How could these people be so selfish? Didn't they care about anything other than their nice lawns and shiny cars? Where would the delinquent kids go if my rezoning application was turned down? To my shock, it was turned down.

4. My "Perfectionist" Phase

I had failed to save the world and join the ranks of the saints, but I wasn't giving up. I decided that I needed to develop higher personal standards, to be more exacting, more detail oriented, more careful and thorough in everything I did. Whether flyspecking a report for commas, cleaning the house down to the last bit of dust, or sacrificing myself for others, I was going to do it "perfectly" or not at all. As a famous actor once said of his film roles: "If it isn't perfect, I'll kill myself." I felt that was the right motto for me.

I had a new job, this time in the development office of a college. A few of my co-workers seemed to join me in working long hours to make sure every fund-raising proposal shone.

They were good, virtuous, true blue. But others were just the opposite—sloppy, careless, mocking. At times, they could be bad, immoral, even vicious.

As hard as I tried, I kept falling behind. I couldn't get all the proposals out on time. What was I to do? Send them out half-baked? The pressure mounted. Finally I broke down in the president's office in tears, as I poured out my heart and tried to explain how much I cared and how I couldn't bear to let the college down by sending out poor work.

I wasn't fired, but more and more people seemed to be begging for my attention at any given time. How could I focus when there were so many needs, and I was the only one who would do the work right, even if it meant working late and Sundays. In the end, it just became too much. I had to quit.

5. My "Compulsive" Phase

At this point, I took a humdrum clerical job that didn't take much thought so that I could concentrate on my private life. It was time to have a little fun. I was still young and full of desires that had been squelched by the endless work of my previous careers.

I had gotten married along the way, which turned out to be a mistake. I wasn't interested in sex with my wife. It was other women I wanted.

Despite having attended a strict Catholic school, I had spent most of my teenage years in a sex trance, and I began to re-experience the same feelings. I had many, many lovers and lied to all of them. Once I had sex with a stranger in a gas station while my wife waited in the car. It got to the point where I would have sex with anyone, sometimes six or more times a night. I was always on the prowl and all of my free time went to the pursuit.

While I was doing this, I also drank too much, and finally landed in a dry-out clinic where the addiction to sex inadvertently popped out. Since my wife was supporting me, I had to give up drink completely on her orders, but I figured out that I could replace it with sedatives and painkillers. The secret was to go to a variety of doctors, none of whom would know about the others.

Then I made a fatal miscalculation. I was on a plane over the Pacific Ocean, on my way to a South Sea Island, when I realized that in the rush to get off I had left my pill box. It was plastic with neat compartments for each of the brightly colored little pills. A few weeks earlier, I had dropped it and the pills had spilled out over the floor but I got down on my hands and knees and feverishly recovered each and every one of them.

Now the pill box was a thousand miles away. A sense of panic swept over me. I started to get the shakes. I was going to have to go through withdrawal, and there was nothing I could do about it. After that I was finished with the pills. I still desired them, but there was too much pain attached to them in my mind.

The Red Years

A s I turned thirty, the red years began. In my youth, I had followed Callicles's advice (in Plato's *Dialogue Gorgias*) that anyone "who would truly live ought to allow personal desires to wax to the uttermost." I was like the Hollywood actress Bette Davis who said in her autobiography that "My passions were all gathered together like fingers that made a fist."

I had wanted and pursued it all: money, success, power, sex, even sainthood. So far it had come to nothing, and I wasn't very happy about that. I felt, deep down, that life had been unfair to me and that many of the people I had encountered had been unfair to me. But it was partly my own fault for letting them mistreat me. It was time to get tough, to get angry, to beat the world into submission.

I know there are people out there who won't approve of these ideas. But they're mostly hypocrites. We all enjoy anger. It's exciting, animating, electrifying. Why do you suppose the news is full of it? Because people want to read about it or see it. And who gets respect? Weaklings? No, strong forceful, ruthless, intimidating types.

6. My "Boss" Phase

My dad had a college friend who built a big drug store chain. When he was over seventy and his wife and eldest son disagreed with a decision of his, he kicked the wife out of the house and the son off his board. Even at his age, he was standing tall. What a role model for me.

I also read about a top lawyer who went in and out of government service and ended up Secretary of Health and Human Services. He was noted for rejecting the first three drafts of any document, for being impatient, sharp-tongued, abrasive, and even abusive at times. He liked to say that "I drive, and drive people, faster than 120 miles an hour."

There was also a powerful US senator around this time, a woman, who was also considered something of a bully and famously said of herself: "I don't get ulcers, I give them." What a great piece of advice! Her staffers did not stay long, but she was feared and had a lot of clout on Capitol Hill.

These people were everything I hadn't been but knew I needed to become. Could I learn to project annoyance, irritation, a short fuse, grouchiness, dissatisfaction, and hostility, at least at work if not at home? Could I learn to criticize, hector, interrupt, nit-pick, disparage, demand, fault-find, finger-point, blame, and intimidate?

As you can see from these questions, I wasn't sure if I could. I had self-doubts. I did try out the "boss" persona a little, but decided that if I were going to get somewhere I had to take my effort to a higher level. So I aborted the "Boss" phase when hardly begun and went on to something even more demanding.

7. My "Fighter" Phase

By now I was working at a law firm. I thought the founder of the firm an ideal person to observe and emulate. He was in his late eighties, cowboy-booted, and at the time I arrived was in a knock-down, drag-out fight with his sixth wife over marital assets. He said he would "kick her ass" and kept referring to her as "El Trampo" before the judge, despite admonitions to stop. He worked nights and weekends on his cases and said that fighting was the only really "fun" thing in life.

The super-lawyer almost met his match in one of his clients. This was a university president, of all things, who was completely obnoxious and wanted to turn any dispute into a bloody brawl. He liked to quote the French philosopher Voltaire who said: "As for myself, weak as I am, I carry on the war to the last moment, I get a hundred pike-thrusts, I return two hundred, and I laugh."*

The other lawyers inside the firm I worked for were almost all hyper-aggressive personalities. The din of their conflicts kept raising the roof, and if any one of them felt scorned, or worse, ignored, he would seethe with indignation before exploding with rage. When end-of-year bonuses were to be decided, the scorpions all crawled out of their offices to devour each other. Since I wasn't a lawyer, I wasn't part of that, but I was nevertheless learning. I "gave as good as I got" in all the battles.

---

* Quoted in William James, *The Varieties of Religious Experience* (New York: Penguin Classics, 1982), 264.

8. My "Avenger" Phase

Before long, I could see that if I wanted to come across as angry and intimidating, I had to take it still further. If people realized that I didn't just want to fight with them, but to humiliate and obliterate them, that I was vindictive as hell, and maybe more than a little sadistic, then I might be able to win the fight even before it started.

First, I had to get my head screwed on tight. I had to understand that life is a winner-take-all struggle. And it isn't just about winners and losers. It is really about masters and slaves. Anyone who dares to challenge you should immediately back off and ask for mercy—or expect to be destroyed. One of our younger female lawyers, who was away for a while working on a successful presidential race, had this attitude down pat. With her, it was always, "If you do this, I'll ruin you." She told me about a White House Chief of Staff who called a cabinet colleague at 5:00 AM (for maximum effect) to say that if he persisted in trying to persuade the President to do something the Chief of Staff didn't like, the latter would "chainsaw your [intimate body part] off." The lawyer added: "He meant it. Even if it took him the rest of recorded history, he wouldn't forget his threat. He would get it done."

I got all this down. Do anything for your allies but don't be too easy with them either, or they will take advantage. They need to acknowledge that you are in control. With everyone else wage a war of utter annihilation. Take your vengeance at every opportunity. I did my best to be an apt student.

9. My "Sulker" Phase

Fighting and avenging take a lot of energy, but you would be surprised how much they energize you too. Still, it is an intense life, and I decided to experiment with other ways to express my anger, my sense that almost everyone around me was unfair to me almost all the time.

What I wanted to explore initially was to drop the aggressive stance and instead come across as cold, uncooperative, resentful, often silent, glowering. I had seen this work for other people. Without having to say or do much, they still controlled the people around them.

I did have my doubts that this more passive approach would work in the law firm, so I switched to a government agency. I congratulated myself on this decision from the start. Here I could do little work, and not give much thought to the work I did, knowing that I could just sullenly glare at my doltish co-workers and brush off anything they said.

I had such high aims and standards in life that what I did at this particular low-level job would hardly matter, and I would not suffer fools gladly. In response, some of my co-workers adopted an unfriendly attitude, but my supervisor was intimidated, and for good reason. I was watching every move she made, jotting down any loose comment, and I was prepared not only to complain to her supervisor, but if necessary to leak to the press—or even sue, which would cause her no end of embarrassment.

All of these people were of course, in their own way, trying to suffocate me. They were jealous of my high intelligence and more refined social graces. But I held them in appropriate contempt. And by continually restraining myself, by hardly saying anything, but also by refusing to cooperate, I exhibited my superiority over all of them.

10. My "Helper" Phase

Outside of work, I was in a somewhat different phase. Throughout my youth, I had seen "helpers" in action, and I was curious about how it felt to be one. My own mother had always been a "helper." She had wanted a girl, so when I arrived, a boy, she dressed me as a girl, put bows in my hair, and always protected me from rough and tumble activities. I got to dress as a boy by age eight, but Mother was always there, sacrificing for me in every imaginable way, and only asking in return that I call her every day and visit as often as possible, something that I would want to do anyway, because I share my life with her in every detail, and because she helps me financially no matter how broke she may be herself.

When I was a teenager, the choirmaster in my Catholic Church kept praising my "beautiful tenor voice." I told him I didn't think I was a tenor, but he responded that he needed tenors, and since he was always befriending and helping me, really became the father I didn't have, I sang as a tenor. It was only much later that I discovered I was, in fact, a baritone.

By now, I had a full understanding that "helping" could be a pretty good way to get others to do what you want and thus a pretty good deal for the "helper." I therefore decided to befriend several people in need, in the same self-sacrificing spirit as my Mother and the priest, and in effect offered to get their lives organized and "improved." In most cases, they turned out to be disappointments, abandoning me at the first opportunity, but one in particular still calls regularly for advice. It feels nice to have someone who looks up to me, who is so devoted to me, and who is willing to do whatever I say.

The Yellow Years

THE GREEN YEARS, throbbing with desires, roughly corresponded to my twenties. The red years, in which I unleashed my anger to get more of what I wanted, but especially to express my sense of injustice at how I was being treated, roughly corresponded to my thirties. There was no particular reason why each stage, with its succession of phases, lasted approximately a decade. It just worked out that way.

As the red years came to a close, I had not the slightest inkling that I would shortly be headed in a new and different direction. It all took me completely by surprise. One day I was driving on an empty highway, in full sunshine, between San Antonio and Austin, Texas. Suddenly I just lost it. My heart started racing. I felt suffocated, as if a band were compressing my chest. My knees and then my whole body shook.

Unable to drive, I pulled off the road. I felt like getting out of the car and running away. But where would I go? Somehow I had to get back behind that wheel and eventually I did. As I continued the drive, I struggled to make sense of what had happened.

When I had been very angry in earlier years, my whole body had been aroused. But I had never felt anything as powerful as the fear that had just gripped me. Worst of all, the fear seemed to have no source. Why had it struck me? What did it signify? I wasn't just fearful and anxious now. I was fearful of being fearful.

I was also consumed with worry about what people would think of me. I was a man. It was socially acceptable for me to be ambitious, to pursue my desires and lusts with gusto, even with abandon. It was socially acceptable to be tough, aggressive, even angry. But to be nervous, worried, panic-stricken? What would people think of me? The more I thought about that, the more nervous and high-strung I became.

11. My "Recluse" Phase

The solution I found for my new state of mind was to move to an isolated cabin about an hour from Wilkes-Barre in the woods of Pennsylvania. There I found that solitude has many uses. At a minimum, it can provide uninterrupted time to work on a project. Or it can provide a much-needed break from the clamor and conflict of the world. As psychologist Carl Rogers has written: "I have come to value highly the privilege of getting away, of being alone. . . ."*

* Carl Rogers, *On Becoming a Person: A Therapist's View of Psychotherapy* (Boston: Houghton Mifflin, 1961), 15.

Even when solitude is not freely chosen, it can provide opportunities, for example to learn a new skill. Singer, songwriter, and musician Bruce Springsteen told the *Washington Post*: "I was someone who grew up in isolation.... I ... mostly lived inside.... I played [musical instruments] for eight hours a day in my room."

In my case, of course, reclusiveness was a response to my new fear, a fear that prompted me to seek safety in being alone. Bruce Springsteen would have understood. Even when wildly successful, he used to retreat:

> You can [be very successful in your career] and everybody applauds you and tells you that you are great. But you can be completely unable at the same time to function in almost every other area [so you withdraw and live as much alone as possible].

Living completely alone now myself, I became much more thoughtful and contemplative despite the underlying high anxiety. I found that my cabin was not only a place to feel safer. It was also a place where I could feel better about myself, like myself more. Indeed it was the only place where my true self could emerge. Anywhere else, the noise and pressure of the world tended to make me self-conscious, formal, and guarded. All the while, I felt phony, foolish, or flibbertigibbeted. Or I watched myself talking too fast or being overbearing or something else inconsistent with what I regarded as my true self.

Like most recluses, I came out of hiding for relatively brief periods. When I did, I liked to become as familiar as possible with the "outside" territory I would be traversing. I recall one time when I forced myself to leave home base for a driving tour of a Central American country with a friend. As each day unfolded, I became edgier. I kept saying things like: "The car agency has probably lost our reservation. Watch out, they will try to cheat us. This car will never make it for a week. We don't have enough gas and there probably aren't any gas stations. Watch out, the car's veering into a drain! Watch out for the potholes! I can't drink this water. These natives look like they are going to rob us. I can't walk barefoot on the beach with all these sharp shells. I'm getting sunburnt. We didn't change enough money, we're sure to run out. Don't eat the shellfish. These mosquitoes are probably malarial. We should have brought medication. The flight out of here will be overbooked and we'll be stranded, etc., etc." My mind only began to slow down when the plane finally touched down at the Philadelphia airport and only stopped entirely when I was back in the safety of my retreat.

I do want to stress that just because I chose to live alone a great deal did not mean that I was inactive, uninvolved, or unproductive. On the contrary, I was extremely busy, full of energy and projects. This reminds me of a novelist friend. He told me that when he first married (to his literary agent after years of living alone), he could not write with his wife in the house. As he said, it made him "jittery." Later, he learned to write with his wife in the same house, but not in the next room. As a result, he continued to be alone for much of the time. But despite this extreme reclusiveness, there was nothing passive or disengaged about him. He is both prolific and admired, just what I hoped and expected to be.

This was all in sharp contrast to my next phase, when my productivity collapsed for unexplained reasons.

12. My "Onlooker" Phase

I wrote a lot in my cabin, and made some money that way, but not enough. In addition, I was tiring of the isolation and thinking that more company would be better for me, so I moved back to the city and took a social services job. Although I was back with people, I still did not feel fully engaged with the world.

Unlike in my cabin, I really didn't want to do anything.

The new job interested me for only a short while. Then I met an attractive woman who made me feel more alive. I made an effort to be charming with her. But that lost its allure too. I stayed in the new job and relationship out of inertia and because I was unwilling to make the effort to extricate myself from either.

When my lady friend accused me to my face of keeping my distance from her, getting to work late, putting off necessary tasks, and generally not getting much done, I responded in several ways. I said that I was trying very hard, was being subjected to an inordinate and undeserved amount of pressure, and would everyone please get off my back! Or I said that the world already had plenty of books, or paintings, or reports, or whatever I was not producing, and does not need any more! Or I said that the task at hand was stupid and boring, well suited for the slavish drones of our consumer society, not for a thoughtful person. Besides, if I threw myself into this particular task, it would leave little time for all the other things I wished to do. In any event, aren't we all speedily heading for the grave? Everything we do is futile. Why make a fuss over nothing?

After these outbursts, I refused to discuss anything further. The last thing I wanted was to become ensnared in the emotional drain of an open conflict, with someone else, or for that matter with myself.

As time went on, I did less and less. I stopped speaking to people, including my friend and/or co-workers. I did as little as possible, bought the minimum amount of groceries, did the minimum amount of cooking, washing, or even changing clothes. Sometimes I would surprise myself with a burst of effort at work, but not at home, or the reverse.

Throughout all this, I was a sincere person. I wasn't my old "gamesman" self. I wasn't trying to deceive or manipulate anyone. I really believed my own ideas about the importance of freedom and of enjoying life before it is too late. Besides, I agreed with psychologist Karen Horney when she said: "It is safer not to try than to try and fail."* What could be more self-evident?

13. My "Conformist" Phase

This was not so much a new phase as an over-lapping phase. I was still an "onlooker" but also a "conformist." Sometimes more the one, sometimes more the other. I wasn't a conformist because I thought I was like other people. Other people could not possibly be so beset by my unattractive anxieties, phobias, or panic attacks. But for this very reason, I wanted to appear to be as much like other people as possible, to try to hide my embarrassing flaws behind a facade of normality and conforming.

---

* Karen Horney, *Neurosis and Human Growth* (New York: W. W. Norton, 1970), 108.

About this time I met a different woman who attracted me and who reinforced my desire to fit in. She had grown up in a wealthy Philadelphia suburb, the daughter of a Presbyterian minister. Although she appeared to be well liked and was included in all the social activities, she felt that the other children, with their expensive toys and clothes and trips and cars, were ridiculing her behind her back as the poor little church girl.

Later, in college, my new lady friend temporarily rebelled against the world of her childhood by dressing as shabbily as possible, cutting her hair very short, wearing extremely unflattering thick black glasses, and associating with a severely bookish crowd. But after graduation, she moved back in with her parents, resumed wearing makeup and attractive if inexpensive clothes, and eventually married a son of one of the church's wealthier families. Thereafter, she bought one of the finest homes in the neighborhood, participated in all the most social charities ranging from the Girl Scouts to the opera, scorned anyone different, and generally settled into an existence identical to everyone else's in the suburb, or at least identical to that of any other wealthy family.

As time passed, "Adele" found it difficult not to show her discomfort and nervousness at social functions. She was always extremely formal and polite, but after a while people criticized her for being too formal and too polite. She was passed over for key volunteer positions with both the Scouts and the opera, in one case because the older women found her "rigid," in the other case because the younger women found her "cold" and "peculiar." She dropped out of both activities, ostensibly to make time for the garden club, but in the end she didn't join the garden club. Her entertaining became rare, so that people began to talk about what she might be doing and how she spent her time. There was a divorce, which was not conforming to expectations, but she still had her big house and money, she needed a male escort and friend, and I was available. We both tried to conform and fit in as best we could, but neither of us could really pull it off. No one ever asked us out.

14. My "Escapist" Phase

As my suburban life, living in my friend's big home, proceeded day by dull day, my mind became increasingly focused on the idea of escape. I read about and was inspired by the writer Paul Bowles. He had been born into a stuffy Long Island family, had fled at age eighteen to Paris, moved through a variety of European and Central American locales for seventeen years, finally settled in Tangier, a Moroccan city where he felt freer. This was an inspiring tale, but I wasn't sure I wanted to settle even in Tangier. In my mind's eye, I saw myself traveling for the rest of my life without ever stopping.

I also read and fantasized about the story of an advertising copywriter who had neither a college nor even a high school degree, but co-founded an advertising agency that soared to the top of its field, and was even named Agency of the Year by *Advertising Age*. He was described by acquaintances as driven, compulsive, completely consumed by his business, and remained so for almost twenty years. But then, suddenly, he quit.

A new, young girlfriend persuaded the former advertising whiz to drive in the Paris-Dakar Rally, a perilous race that no American had ever finished. After a year of planning and hundreds of thousands of dollars in expenses, he literally ran out of gas in Niger. Thereafter, he dabbled in filmmaking and a writing career ("It didn't pay . . . well enough."), joined a Democratic presidential nominee as creative chief of advertising, but found that most of his ideas were rejected.

He next moved to London with a new girlfriend, but "nothing [led] to anything [because I] wanted it that way—no commitments." When that proved disappointing ("I realized the very thing I . . . wanted was making me nuts."), he decided to return to advertising, but startled his former colleagues in Manhattan by joining a regional agency in the South. Eight months later, he abandoned this new firm and his 1600 horsepower speedboat to move back to Manhattan and start yet another agency.

I loved reading stories like this. I wanted to throw everything over and escape too. I was a little bit afraid to do it, but I also thought that once on the road all my anxieties would slip off me like the skin of a snake and I would be my old self again and free. Meanwhile I could savor it in anticipation.

Unfortunately, I never did escape. I worried about money. I worried that as the years passed, the life of continuous travel or change would become routinized, burdensome, lonely, even, as the Roman philosopher Seneca warned, a kind of "slavery."* I pondered "Ithaca," the often quoted poem by Greek poet Constantine Cavafy, describing the utter futility of seeking new lands.

15. My "Routinist" Phase

If I had become intermittently an "onlooker," a "conformist," and an "escapist" (at least in my mind), I was also a "routinist." I tried to control anxiety by sticking rigidly to routine.

It was no surprise to me that Cavafy had described the futility of escapism. Look at his own life. He had buried himself in the same repetitive behavior, day in and day out, without a break, without any relief or escape, except in the world of his poetry. Despite his intelligence and literary gifts, he not only chose to remain in the same modest job in the Alexandrian waterworks department. He

---

* Seneca, *Letters From a Stoic*, translated by Robin Campbell (New York: Penguin Classics, 1969), 189.

also occupied the same walk-up apartment for most of his adult life.

Cavafy reminded me of my best friend in high school. A Jewish boy, he had been out of place in the Catholic School we both attended, chosen by his parents because it was the only "good" school in town, but unwelcoming to non-Christians, especially one who was brilliant, bookish, and loved to write poetry. At one point, he stormed at his parents that he could not stand another day at this school, but was made to go back against all his tears and protests. Later, at Yale, he became a campus radical and activist, was almost expelled for defying the school's rules, and then suffered an incapacitating nervous breakdown. Thereafter, the once sensitive poet and fiery rebel took a laboratory job with a major utility company, married a woman of fixed habits, settled into an immutable routine, and was never heard from again by his former friends.

What Cavafy, my young Jewish friend—and eventually I—wanted from routinism, with its insistence on the repetitive and familiar, was some control over our lives, and especially some control over our fears. Above all, we wanted to sidestep risks, which exacerbated the fears and anxieties. But by trying to eliminate risk-taking, we often found that even the smallest, irreducible risk, such as leaving one's home without an umbrella, or walking under the sun without a hat, became nearly unbearable.

As my yellow years stretched out to another decade and I neared fifty, I felt increasingly frustrated, wistful, and immobilized. I sensed there would be another turn in the road, but was unsure what it would be.

The Blue Years

I HAD EXPERIENCED THE years of throbbing desire, of volcanic anger, of incessant fear and anxiety. Why did I not anticipate that years of sadness, of serious depression, would follow? I knew all about depression. A friend of mine had sunk into gloom shortly after college. I told him: "Pull up your socks. Get out of the apartment." But he would just respond: "I'll go brush my teeth," and in a moment he would nod off and wake at the end of the next day. Then he would try to get up but couldn't decide what underwear to put on or whether he had lost his toothbrush.

Depression isn't all bad. It does stop us in our tracks. In effect, we are forced to rethink our life. But as usual, I overdid it. I spent yet another decade exploring all sorts of blue moods, working through them concurrently or consecutively. I lived the blue life to the full. However hard it was, I lived to tell the tale.

16. My "Defendant" Phase

I was still living in the very fancy suburban home owned by my lady friend, feeling increasingly guilty about my shortcomings, basically ashamed of myself. It seemed that I couldn't do anything right. I also knew myself to be clumsy. Why then did I carry a big hammer into the living room? I intended to hammer down a nail that had popped up in the floor. But in that case what brought me in the vicinity of the prized antique bowl that sat on the Ming side table, and what possessed me to drop the hammer right there and shatter the bowl?

After doing that I was tortured. I couldn't get the incident out of my mind. As a result, nothing was safe from me. Either I had to leave this house or have it child-proofed, as if for an infant.

After that, the remorse and self-reproach really escalated. I couldn't shake it. It was shameful and humiliating to be such a failure, and even more shameful and humiliating to admit it to myself and others.

17. My "Prisoner" Phase

I sunk even lower in my own self-estimation as feelings of hopelessness and helplessness overwhelmed me. I felt trapped in a dungeon of my own making with no possible escape. By now, I sat, day by day, hardly ever rising from my chair in a cheap, walk-up apartment. I had barely enough money to pay my modest expenses. Now well into my fifties, I was sure nobody would ever be interested in me. Life had passed me by, there was no longer any point to having ambitions, trying anything new, taking any risks. Indeed, there was no reason to leave the apartment except for some occasional grocery shopping. I just sat in the gloom of my increasingly shabby and dusty room.

I hardly ever read, but found some solace in the Russian novelist and philosopher Leo Tolstoy. He too had experienced this emptiness. He had written of the moment when

> something had broken within me on which my life had always rested, [so] that I had nothing left to hold onto. . . . This took place at a time when, so far as . . . outer circumstances went, I ought to have been completely happy. I had a good wife who loved me and whom I loved; good children and a large property, which was increasing with no pains taken on my part. I was more respected . . . than I had ever been. . . . Without exaggeration I could believe my name

> already famous. . . . Yet [all at once]
> I could give no reasonable meaning
> to any actions of life. . . .*

What a contrast to my own life, which had been a complete failure. But even Tolstoy, born into wealth and crowned by such golden triumphs, had come to feel as I did, crushed and empty. I occasionally told myself that Tolstoy and I felt this way because we were more sensitive, more deeply feeling, more attuned to the deep rhythms of the universe than other people. Occasionally I thought of myself as a character in a play of tragic dimensions, at least a Blanche Dubois, if not a Hamlet. But mostly I just felt stuck, inert. And I knew that my passivity, aimlessness, ambivalence, and procrastination would only make matters worse. I was completely unable to stir myself, to make any firm decisions, to take any decisive action. When I shattered the antique bowl on

---

* William James, *The Varieties of Religious Experience* (New York: Penguin Classics, 1982), 153–154.

the Ming table, I could at least feel guilt that something went so wrong. Now I just took for granted that everything would forever be wrong, and I was absolutely powerless to affect the outcome.

Surprisingly, that was not true. There was more ahead. My blue years weren't finished with me.

18. My "Dependent" Phase

The suburban matron took me back. Who knows why? I offered to pay a few bills, as I had always done, in addition to my own personal expenses, but this time it was waved aside. Some investment had paid off big. My friend said she couldn't imagine me, depressed as I had been, paying for anything. Lavish meals out, free film and theater, fancy clothes (so I could dress to her standard), free trips all followed.

I talked about finding work, but never took a step in that direction. I slept late, hung out at the gym a lot, the hair stylist, shopped a lot, took cooking lessons to use when the cook was off.

Some of my old friends criticized this arrangement, but I told them I was a loving, caring person who simply put the needs and convenience of my lady friend ahead of my own. I just wanted to create a restful, soothing environment for her when she returned from her charities, and what was wrong with that?

In addition to paying the bills, my friend also made the decisions. She even told me when to eat or when to go to bed. She said she knew best what was good for me. Perhaps she did, but I was too old for this. And, increasingly, I felt that she was being tightfisted, that I had to ask for every single penny. Anyway, it didn't matter. I was about to meet another woman who would sweep me off my feet and put me in a new direction.

19. My "Self-Effacer" Phase

One day, at the local gourmet food shop, I met a slightly older woman, an attorney. She invited me to have coffee and later to have dinner at her home. I found this woman to be everything I was not: strong, forceful, energetic, willful, aggressive, full of ideas and ambitions. Just to be around her made life exciting. Before long, I left the suburban matron and moved in with my exciting, new love.

"Louise" joked to an acquaintance that "men are just like horses or dogs. You have to break and train them." At first, she made small demands on me: "Honey, bring me a glass of soda. . . . Honey, go to the store and buy me some cleaning supplies. . . . Honey, I'm tired, won't you clean the house and make dinner?" In a way, this was a relief. Unlike at the rich matron's, I had a role to play, something to do. But, over time, the commands grew shriller, more critical, even insulting: "You didn't put enough ice in this soda. Why did you take so long getting those supplies from the store? This house is a pigpen. What's wrong with you? Can't you see this dirt, can't you do anything without my having to tell you?"

On Tuesday and Wednesday nights, "Louise" went out with her friends. She insisted that I wait for her alone. She was often with other men, but I was never supposed to be alone with another woman. Each Sunday evening, she invited to dinner her own mother and brothers, despite constant feuding with them. My own relatives and former friends were not welcome in the house, nor did she approve of me seeing them anywhere else.

As time passed, I felt so isolated that I had more trouble than usual in thinking for myself. I sensed that something was wrong but blamed myself. I thought: "Deep down I am just as lazy, inconsiderate, and worthless as this woman says I am. I cannot go back to living alone, I would be lost. I have to try harder to please her."

I began to be torn by feelings of love and hate, of desperately wanting to be free and wanting to capitulate and be completely controlled, of thinking "Louise" was godlike and thinking she was a beast.

To win a little freedom, I began to lie, at first occasionally, then frequently. I lied so often I couldn't remember the truth anymore. And I procrastinated. Even the simplest job now took me days. This made "Louise" angry and sometimes even led to violence.

Finally, feeling utterly worthless but fearing for my life, I fled.

20. My "Martyr" Phase

I had been through a lot. But somehow I landed on my feet and found some work at a bank. It wasn't very challenging, but knowing that I was supporting myself again made me feel better. Whatever else could be said of me, I was a survivor.

I worked hard, harder than any time since my twenties, and got a raise. Then a promotion. Managers at the bank increasingly depended on me. And I took pleasure in helping everybody and doing such a good job.

The only criticism I ever heard was that I was a bit grim. I have to admit that there is some truth to that, but I wouldn't call it "grim." I would call it "serious" or "businesslike." What is wrong with that? Life is no bed of roses; the only sensible response is to do our duty and make the best of it. At this moment in my life, if someone knocked on my door and told me I had won a gigantic lottery prize, I would look at them in the eye and reply: "This is sure to complete the ruin of my life."

It wasn't that I can't grasp the concept of fun. I acknowledge that fun is normal—so long as we understand that there is always a heavy price to be paid for it. Hard work, doing what you ought to do, helping others, self-sacrifice is what it's really all about, not fun, and while I don't want to lecture my co-workers, I also don't want to involve myself in their frivolities.

At a recent business meeting, I told my colleagues that I had spent the Thanksgiving holiday preparing the business plan they would see. I also mentioned that I had awakened at 2:00 AM the previous night to put the final touches on it. But even so I sincerely asked them not to hold back any criticism. When a department head told me that she would take on several new assignments "Even though my husband is talking about divorcing me, my widowed father is moving into a nursing home this week, and I will have to miss my daughter's ballet performance for the fourth time," I knew that I had found a kindred spirit.

After all the stormy seas I have crossed, I feel that I have finally grown up. Other people are children or want to act like children, show little regard for responsibilities, or the welfare of others. Despite their behavior, I try to remain calm and never, ever, raise my voice in anger. My aim is to be unselfish and thoughtful at all times, and gently prod or remind those who stray from the straight path. If I am almost always overwhelmed, exhausted, unable to complete the endless series of tasks I have taken on, this is because others are not pitching in, are not living up to the same standard, so that there is always much more to do than I possibly can do.

I think of this as a very realistic and practical approach, but I do worry if it really is realistic and practical. I worry about burning out. And the more I worry about burning out, the more depressed I feel, which drains me of the energy I need.

The one thing I allow myself is a little self-pity. I think it is therapeutic and not something to be ashamed of. Like anything else, it can be done well or badly, and I do it well, with even a little panache.

Do I Want to Be Happy?

THIS IS A question I occasionally ask myself. So far, of course, there hasn't been a lot of what most people would call happiness in my life. There has been a lot of living, many experiences, and many lessons learned.

Do I really care? If I haven't found happiness up to this point, should I care? Do I want it in the future? I doubt it.

But, first of all, what is happiness? Based on my own fleeting experiences of it in the past, I would say that it is an emotional state. In this sense, it is like desire, anger, fear, and sadness—just one more big emotional state that we can experience. Logically, it would follow that to arrive at happiness, we would have to turn down the burners of desire, anger, fear, and sadness, burners turned so high and hot in my own life that they have been fairly scorching.

This has been the advice of numerous sages over the course of human history. Keep these powerful emotions in constant check, they say, lest they burst into flame and consume us. Many people disagree of course, especially about moderating our desires. We have already mentioned Callicles's advice to "let personal desires wax to the uttermost." The philosopher Isaiah Berlin said that moderating our desires was just "sour grapes" thinking.* This is in contrast to the Buddha, who taught in the *Dhammapada* that "From craving

---

* Isaiah Berlin, *Two Concepts of Liberty* (Oxford: Clarendon Press, 1958).

arises sorrow," or Albert Einstein, who agreed with the Buddha that "I am happy because I want nothing." *

What if we followed the advice of the Buddha and Einstein, and sought to tune down our desires into mere preferences? What traits, what experiences would we expect to follow? I have read a lot about this, and here is how one author tries to distill the experience of happiness (next page):†

---

* For more on this, see Hunter Lewis, *A Question of Values: Six Ways We Make the Personal Choices* (New York: Harper & Row, 1990), 154.

† *The Beguiling Serpent: A Re-evaluation of Emotions and Values* (Mt. Jackson,VA: Axios Press, 2000), 25.

absorbed
accepting • active
affectionate • approving
aware • benign • comfortable
committed • compassionate • confident
contented • curious • empathetic • energetic
flexible • focused • forgiving • friendly • full of humor
generous • genuine • grateful • happy • imperturbable
interested • joyful • loving • modest • nonjudgmental
open • patient • peaceful • playful • realistic
refreshed • relaxed • respectful • serene
sincere • stimulated • supple
sympathetic • steady • tolerant
tranquil • unhurried
unselfconscious
warm

The common theme in all these traits and feelings, we are told, is that we are supposed to feel more connected, connected to people, to work, and to the world. Being social creatures, we are supposed to like this feeling of connection. Well, I don't deny that strong desires, anger, fear, or sadness tend to disconnect us from others, from the world.

But let's not overstate the pleasure of feeling connected. Often we need to disconnect and disconnect fast, such as when we are chased by a dangerous animal or a criminal. Under those circumstances, it is disconnect (and scram) or die. It's true that the wild animals are few these days, but there is no shortage of predatory humans.

Besides, it isn't clear that the traits and feelings associated with happiness by the know-it-all author I quoted above are all that great. The same author has to admit that there are two sides to this story:

> [A demanding sort of person] might argue that feelings of calm are for

retirees, feelings of cheerfulness or connectedness are for children, that seeking to be calm, cheerful, and connected will interfere with what really matters in life, getting ahead. . . . [Alternatively, the same] individual . . . may concede that a calm, cheerful, and connected attitude makes us more popular or successful with others and then conclude that the answer is simply to fake such an attitude. In this vein, a twenty-seven-year-old wholesale meat dealer explained to a *Washington Post* reporter that appearing to have a sense of humor makes picking up girls easier: "You've got to be able to make them laugh, if you don't you can't pick [them up]. You make 'em laugh, you got 'em. That's the bottom line." [In a different vein, an angry person] might argue that life is just constant warfare, a matter of destroy or be destroyed, and that calm and connected states will just render one vulnerable to [exploitation].*

Let's also keep in mind that if we want to be happy, we have to make some real sacrifices. For example, we can no longer insist on having everything exactly as we want, the principal theme of desire. We can no longer fire ourselves up with the notion that life and other people are unfair to us, the principal theme of anger. We can no longer nourish our pride, or worry so much about how we are coming across to others, the principal theme of fear in today's complicated social world. And we can no longer afford to dwell on the irrecoverable losses we have suffered or the unforgivable mistakes we have made, the principal themes of sadness. In general, we must utterly abandon self-pity and all the related consolations that it brings.

---

* *The Beguiling Serpent*, 29.

This assumes that we even have a choice about any of this. Do we have a choice about our emotional life? Some people think we do. For example, here is the know-it-all author again:

> Our emotional states . . . represent choices. . . . The reason we have chosen [troublesome] . . . emotions is not because it makes us feel good, but rather because we have been taught, either by individuals or by circumstances, or have taught ourselves in bygone times, that this is the way we should feel. Furthermore, because most people have little or no idea that they have such choices—let alone how these choices are made— they are as bound into their condition as if they had no choice at all; it is as if they were locked in a cell. It is not exactly a cell of their own making, as various New Agers might like to tell them; yet it's a cell whose

> door is not really locked. All that
> is required is to know that one can
> open the door and walk out.*

Well, if we do have a choice, I choose not to try to be happy. If I am living in a cell of my own making, I'll stay in it. It doesn't feel like a cell to me. It feels like a rejection of the cell most people live in or aspire to, the cell of normality. I don't want to be like all those other people. I consider myself special, and I want to lead a special life.

A close friend once said of the famous French fashion designer, Yves. St. Laurent:

> Deep down [the designer is] tortured
> and tormented. But he wouldn't
> change his situation for all the gold
> in the world. He . . . wants . . . to be
> what he is, rather than some guy with
> a normal life.†

---

* Ibid., 43–44.

† Betty Catrou, *W Magazine*, (Fall, 1973): 58.

To which I say: Bravo, Yves. As for myself, I am not about to sacrifice my favorite activity of all, self-pity. I would rather perfect it, shine it to a high sheen. That would be a singular goal as the world sees things, but I am a singular person.

I have no doubt that some people, many people, will dismiss me. They will regard my life as pitiful. But I think the greater pity is not the way I have behaved, but the way I have been treated by others, and in particular how little I have been appreciated. Over and over, I have tried my best to help others. Who has paid the slightest attention? Who has ever really thanked me?

I don't deny for a moment that this is self-pity. There is a purity to self-pity. And an honesty. Who knows where my life may lead me to next? Perhaps after perfecting self-pity, I will, after all, in the end, make my peace with happiness. There have been so many twists and turns in my journey that nothing can completely surprise me. Don't, however, hold your breath. I do not wish to be like everyone else. And what could be more pitifully ordinary than the hope for happiness?

Appendix
The Five Basic Emotions

1. Desire

Some General Characteristics of People Embracing "Desire":

- Acquisitive
- Addicted
- Demanding
- Extremely ambitious
- Fixated
- Obsessed
- Selfish
- Willful

Some Characteristic Behavioral Strategies Associated with "Desire":

- ◆ Gamesman or woman
- ◆ Prince or princess
- ◆ High flyer
- ◆ Compulsive
- ◆ Perfectionist

The Central Theme of "Desire":

- ◆ "Things absolutely must be one way and one way only (my way)."

2. Anger

Some General Characteristics of People Embracing "Anger":

- ◆ Angry
- ◆ Bad-tempered
- ◆ Controlling
- ◆ Domineering
- ◆ Explosive
- ◆ Grouchy

- Hostile
- Hyper-critical
- Impatient

Some Characteristic Behavioral Strategies Associated with "Anger":

- Boss
- Fighter
- Avenger
- Sulker
- "Helper"

The Central Theme of "Anger":

- "Life and other people are unfair to me."

3. Fear

Some General Characteristics of "Fear":

- Anxious
- Fearful
- Eccentric
- "High strung"

- Isolated
- Mistrustful
- Nervous
- Panicked
- Terrified

Some Characteristic Behavioral Strategies Associated with "Fear":

- Recluse
- Onlooker
- Conformist
- Escapist
- Routinist

The Central Theme of "Fear":

- "It will be an unbearable blow to my pride if people think badly of me."

4. Sadness

Some General Characteristics of "Sadness":

- Alienated
- Ashamed
- Dependent

- ◆ Depressed
- ◆ Embarrassed
- ◆ Guilty
- ◆ Hopeless
- ◆ Sad
- ◆ Terrified

Some Characteristic Behavioral Strategies Associated with "Sadness":

- ◆ Defendant
- ◆ Prisoner
- ◆ Dependent
- ◆ Self-effacer
- ◆ Martyr

The Central Theme of "Sadness":

- ◆ "I will never recover from this loss and/ or I have made a completely unforgivable mistake."

5. Happiness

Some General Characteristics of "Happy" People. They Feel:

- Appreciative
- Calm
- Cheerful
- Clear-headed
- Comfortable
- Confident
- Contented
- Joyful
- Peaceful
- Playful
- Refreshed
- Relaxed
- Secure
- Tranquil
- Untroubled

In Their Relations with Others, They Are:

- Accepting
- Affectionate

- Compassionate
- Empathetic
- Forgiving
- Friendly
- Inclusive
- Loving
- Nonjudgmental (of others' motives)
- Open
- Patient
- Respectful
- Sincere
- Sympathetic
- Tolerant

Others Observe Them to Be:

- Absorbed
- Balanced
- Energetic
- Flexible
- Focused
- Full of humor
- Interested

- Realistic
- Unhurried

The Central Theme of "Happiness":

- "I feel connected to other people, to my work, and to the world."